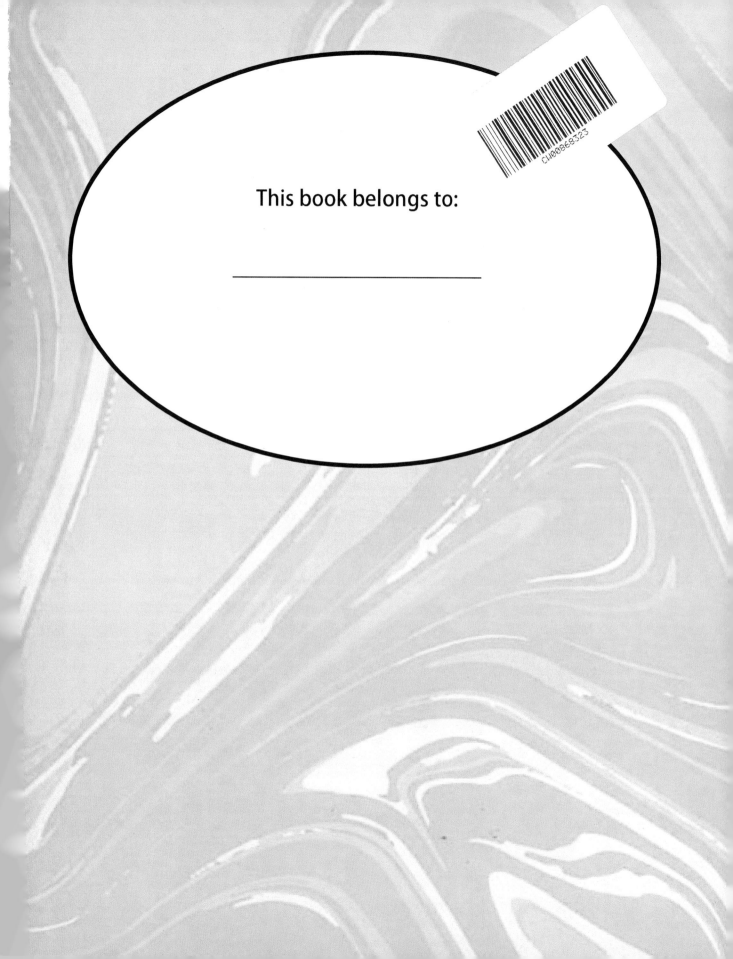

This book belongs to:

_____

Written by Beth Logan
Illustrated and designed by Beth Logan

ISBN: 9798595801850

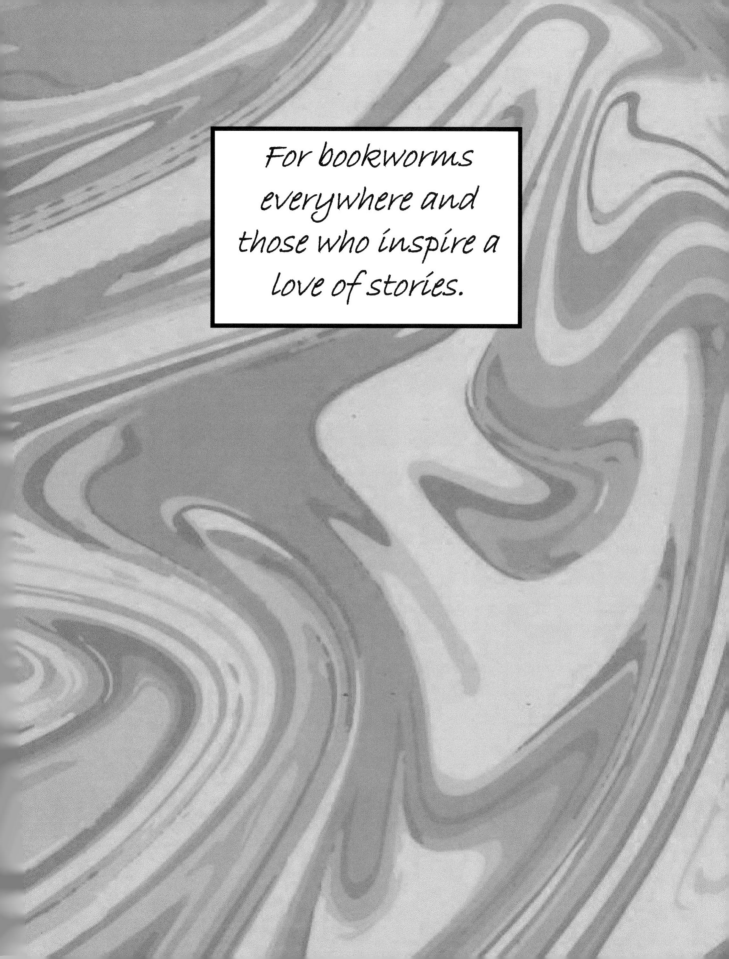

For bookworms everywhere and those who inspire a love of stories.

I have a little bookworm- he arrived from Bookworm Land.
We are the best of buddies; he snuggles in my hand.

He stands on the shelves- around the books he'll linger.
He likes nothing better than to perch upon my finger!

He is there when I need him, to choose a favourite book and helps me turn the pages whilst I read and look.

We read along together- about dragons, about kings, about journeys, about people and AMAZING things!

About famous buildings in the world and towers very tall.

About elephants and lions and insects very small.

Creatures who crawl on land, birds who sing in trees, fishes who swim and giant mammals in the seas.

We learn about planets, in the galaxy, far up in the sky:
the yellow sun, the pearly moon and clouds that float on high.

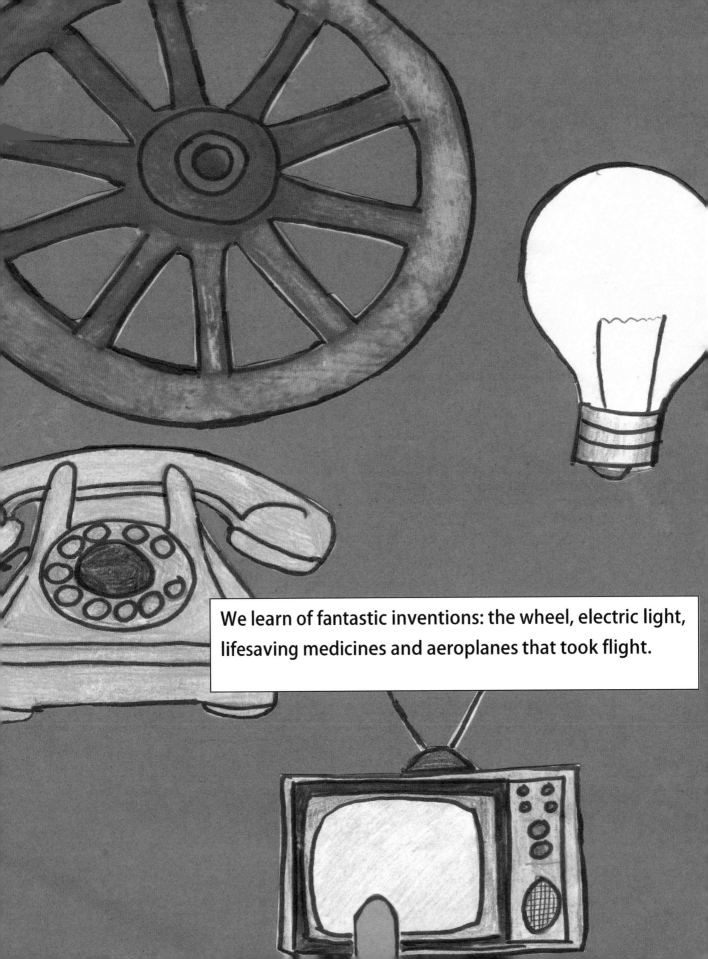

We learn of fantastic inventions: the wheel, electric light, lifesaving medicines and aeroplanes that took flight.

He likes to climb mountains of books- it takes him quite a while, to finally reach the summit at the top of the pile!

When I start to do my sums, I really have to say:
'Dearest bookworm, I am trying to count and you are in my way!'

He keeps my pens and pencils company and watches whilst I write.

He listens to my bedtime stories, before I say goodnight.

My baby brother borrowed him and kept him for some time.
He took him to the nursery to read a nursery rhyme.

But, good news quickly came for my cheeky little brother,
when who should come in the evening post... Surprise! Surprise! Another!

This bookworm is just like the other one, cheerful, long and thin.

In fact, I am correct in saying, he is my bookworm's twin!

They often hide together, huddled out of sight,
then pop out suddenly to give someone a fright!

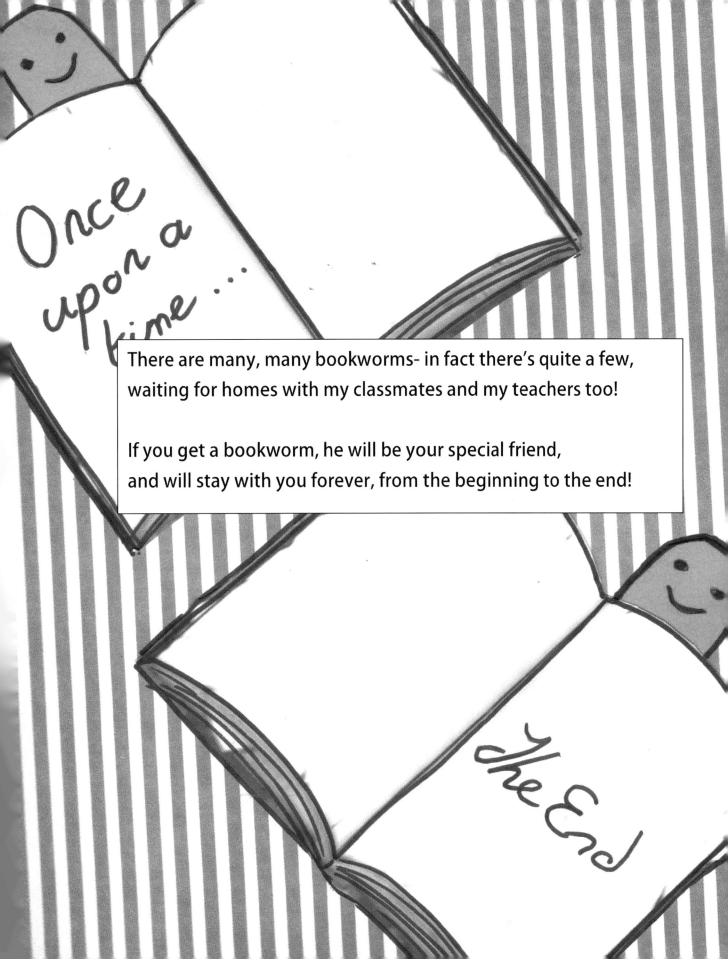

There are many, many bookworms- in fact there's quite a few,
waiting for homes with my classmates and my teachers too!

If you get a bookworm, he will be your special friend,
and will stay with you forever, from the beginning to the end!

Printed in Great Britain
by Amazon

56503701R00015